The Fire

ANNETTE GRIESSMAN

illustrated by LEONID GORE

G. P. PUTNAM'S SONS • NEW YORK

For the firefighters—A. G.

To Kathy Dawson and Cecilia Yung,
with whom I would fight any fire—L. G.

G. P. PUTNAM'S SONS
A division of Penguin Young Readers Group
Published by The Penguin Group
Penguin Group (USA) Inc., 375 Hudson Street, New York, NY 10014, U.S.A.
Penguin Group (Canada), 10 Alcorn Avenue, Toronto, Ontario, Canada M4V 3B2
(a division of Pearson Penguin Canada Inc.).
Penguin Books Ltd, 80 Strand, London WC2R 0RL, England.
Penguin Ireland, 25 St. Stephen's Green, Dublin 2, Ireland (a division of Penguin Books Ltd.).
Penguin Group (Australia), 250 Camberwell Road, Camberwell, Victoria 3124, Australia
(a division of Pearson Australia Group Pty Ltd).
Penguin Books India Pvt Ltd, 11 Community Centre, Panchsheel Park, New Delhi - 110 017, India.
Penguin Group (NZ), Cnr Airborne and Rosedale Roads, Albany, Auckland 1310, New Zealand
(a division of Pearson New Zealand Ltd).
Penguin Books (South Africa) (Pty) Ltd, 24 Sturdee Avenue, Rosebank, Johannesburg 2196, South Africa.
Penguin Books Ltd, Registered Offices: 80 Strand, London WC2R 0RL, England.

Published simultaneously in Canada. Manufactured in China by South China Printing Co. Ltd.
Designed by Cecilia Yung and Katrina Damkoehler. Text set in AT Administer Book.
The art was done in acrylic and pastel on paper.

Library of Congress Cataloging-in-Publication Data
Griessman, Annette. The fire / Annette Griessman ; illustrated by Leonid Gore.   p. cm.
Summary: When their house is destroyed by fire and everything is lost except a stuffed bear
and a family photograph, Mama reminds Maria and her little brother, Pepito,
that they still have their most important possessions.
[1. Fires—Fiction. 2. Family life—Fiction. 3. Hispanic Americans—Fiction.]
I. Gore, Leonid, ill. II. Title.   PZ7.G881235Fi 2005   [E]—dc22   2003024449

ISBN 0-399-24019-5
10 9 8 7 6 5 4 3 2 1   First Impression

It is evening, and Mama is making soup. My little brother, Pepito, colors a truck in shades of red. I hold Niña on my lap and let her watch Mama stir with her big wooden spoon. Niña may be just a stuffed bear, but she loves Mama's soup as much as I do.

Mama is humming. Pepito is coloring. And Niña is soft in my arms.

It is then that I smell it.

"Mama," I say, "is the soup burning?"

As Mama starts to turn, I see it. A thin wisp of smoke curling in from the hall. Mama sees it too, and her eyes get very wide.

"Stay here, Maria. Keep your brother safe," she says.

Then she dashes into the hallway faster than I have ever seen her run.

I have a funny feeling in my stomach, like it is made
of a hundred rubber bands. I want Mama to come back.
"Mama!" says Pepito. He gets up and starts to run.
I grab his hand, hard, and hold him here with me.
"No, Pepito, no!"

The hallway starts to glow. It is not like the glow
of the moon or a night-light. This glow flickers and dances
as if it were alive. The smoke flows into the room like a snake
in the air. It fills my nose and throat and makes them feel hot.

I am now afraid. I can tell Pepito is, too, by the way
his hand trembles.

"Mama!" he calls again, and this time I call with him.
"Mama! Mama!"
When she does not come, I pull Pepito to the floor,
under the smoke, and we start to crawl for the door.
I know that we should get out.

Then, a dark shape slips out of the flickering glow and becomes our mama. Her face is dirty, but underneath, her cheeks are pale. "Run, children, run!" she gasps. "The house is on fire. Run!"

My legs feel wobbly, but I run with Mama and Pepito. We run very fast out into the night.

Pepito and I stand on the cool grass while Mama pounds on the door of Mr. Ortez. Mama is telling him about the fire, but I can't listen. All I can do is stare at the house with tears in my eyes.

I have left Niña, my Niña, behind.

By the time the fire trucks come, I can see flickering in every window. Smoke curls into the air and blots out the stars.

The lights from the fire trucks flicker too, but it is a good kind of flicker and it makes me feel safe.

As Mama hugs Pepito and me, we watch the firemen
pour out of the trucks like an army.
The flickers inside the house brighten and a long ribbon
of flame breaks out of one window. The firemen pull out their
hoses, and the battle begins.

Water sprays. Voices shout. Feet pound. Engines roar.
And everywhere, red lights flicker.
For a while it seems as if the firemen will win.
Then there is a crash and Mama says, "Oh, no!" in a voice
that shakes.

That's when I see the roof fall in.

The water sprays like a glittering fountain, but I know it will do no good. Flames shoot into the sky like hungry tongues, trying to eat the night.

I hear Mama crying and I am surprised to hear that I am crying too. Pepito stares at the fire, but I think he is too small to understand.

It is gone. All gone. The stove. The soup. The coloring book. My Niña.

All gone. Everything is gone, and nothing will ever be the same.

Water continues to spray, and at last the flames die down.

Mama wipes tears from her eyes as a figure steps out of the flickering lights. "I'm sorry, ma'am. All we could save were these."

The fireman is holding a framed picture in one hand, and he is holding my Niña in the other! I snatch her from his hand and hold her tight. Her fur is soft against my cheek.

My mama takes the picture from the fireman, and for a moment she is quiet. The fireman, Pepito, and I are quiet too.

"Thank you," says Mama, smiling at the fireman. "Thank you very much. Everything is safe now."

"Mama!" I cry. "Everything isn't safe now! Everything is gone!"

My mama kneels down between Pepito and me, and her eyes are deep and full of love. "First, my dear Maria, the fireman saved Niña, did he not?"

I clutch my bear tight.

"Yes, he saved Niña," I say. "But Niña is not everything."

"Second," says my mama, "he saved this." She holds out the picture.

It is a picture from a shelf in the kitchen. I recognize it, but feel like I am looking at it for the very first time.

"The picture reminds me of what I have. This," she says, pointing at the picture, "is everything."

She touches each figure in the picture. "Mama, Pepito, Maria . . ."

"And Niña," I add, tucking Niña up under my chin.

"And Niña," she says with a smile. Mama pulls Pepito and me close. I take a deep breath and feel the rubber bands in my stomach relax.

I look at Pepito, I look at Mama, and I feel Niña in my arms, and I know Mama is right.

The fire came and took our home—but it didn't take everything.